My Name is Mitzi

Frank J. Kopet

This book is a biographical novella featuring our dear pup Mitzi. Most of the events, places, times, people and animals are real – the rest is my imagination.

What ever you can do
Or dream you can do
Begin it
Boldness has genius
Power and Magic in it
Gothe

My Name is Mitzi
Is dedicated to
My best friend
My life companion
My beautiful wife
Marie

My Name is Mitzi

My name is Mitzi. As you can see from my picture on the cover of this book, I am a small, two-year-old, dog. I was born on May 15, 2016 in Cocoa Beach, Florida.

From the time I could interpret people-talk, I kept hearing words that said I'm a pretty little dog. Well, that's what I heard, so I guess they know something about a dog being pretty – whatever that is.

In my doggy world, we have a great interest in how you, and my kind, smell. My nose is always in motion, and seeking a scent. Maybe being pretty is the same as having an exciting odor.

My Mom and Dad smell great, so, I guess that means they must be pretty.

From what I know, whether we are big or small, all doggy-fingers and toes are very short – short but very useful. I can run and dig and hold what needs holding. Grasping a pencil to write or utilizing a keyboard to type is impossible. That means I can't use a computer. All of these can't-do items have no relevance because, I can't read either.

So how did my Mom and Dad help me with the telling of my story? It's very simple. It didn't take very long for us to know that we have a special ability. When speaking in our own language, we all can understand, most of what is said to each other. So for my story, I'm telling Mom and Dad what to write, and they do the rest.

At times, they misinterpret translating from my doggy yips, grrrs, and wruffs to English. And sometimes it is very difficult for me to understand the meaning of their English words. That's when I react by tilting my head in question, and then wait to hear more.

Working together is a lot of fun. When Mom or Dad reads back what they think I said, and many times it is all wrong, we all giggle, and I roll on the floor in a fit of laughter. In due time, we usually get something that's close to defining my doggy talk. Keep in mind I said, usually.

Just so we all know, and everyone should recognize, that I admit goofs exist within my book. It's difficult to catch them all. And of course I forgive Mom and Dad for twisting some of the facts.

Casper

I suppose we should stop for a minute and let me explain a little more about who I am, and about my unique heritage. As you know, my Mom and Dad are not my birth parents. I remember a white silky haired canine, named Casper. He is my father; and he is a mixed-breed Maltese – Shih Tzu. As it is with my father, my birth mother, Dory, is also a mixed breed Maltese.

Her mom is a pure Maltese and her dad a full bred Pomeranian.

Maybe that's why people say I'm pretty. I am half Maltese, part Shih Tzu, and part Pomeranian. I have a little of something from the very best.

Now let's get back to my humans: my adopted Mom and Dad. Allow me to tell you about when we first met.

Mitzi - 3 weeks

During the middle of every morning my pack is back in our whelping kennel taking a nice nap. We, my brothers and sisters, are tired from playing and we're all jumbled together into a nice meld of puppies.

I didn't hear them come in, nor did I hear them talking. All I can remember is Shannon, my breeder, picking me up from the warmth and comfort of my brothers and sisters and putting me into my Dad's arms. I'm barely awake, and it was kind of scary.

For those first moments, I was very anxious and afraid. Though frightened, I realized Dad was very careful. He cuddled and *hugged* me into his body and then up to his face. I thought he *kissed* me. Maybe he was sniffing me. It didn't matter. His warmth and the newness of his scent made me want to snuggle my nose into the crook of his arm. Oh, it felt so good to be pulled in tight and safe. I could stay that way forever.

Although I wanted to cuddle, it didn't last very long. When I felt really comfortable and secure, he nudged me away. I felt like I was hanging in the air until he placed me into my Mom's gentle hands. As you know, I call them my Mom and Dad but at that time I didn't know who they were, or that I was going to be part of their pack. Oops, I guess I should leave doggy-words out of this epic and say Mom and Dad are my family.

Mitzi - 8 weeks

Back to my story: I found out much later they were here to see me and the rest of my brothers and sisters. As I was saying my Mom held me close to her, but not as tight as Dad. She was gentle, and I felt a new kind of *love*. She kissed me on the top of my head and looked directly into my eyes. That was a big surprise. She showered me with pure people-love.

What I really expected were a couple of juicy licks to clean my face – and some of my other parts which I shall leave to your imagination.

Anyway, her eyes sparkled. She had a beautiful smile. I stuck out my tongue. Not out of disrespect but I wanted to give her a nice lick – it didn't work. I was too far away. I squirmed and tried to nuzzle-in to get comfortable. My Dad saw me wiggling and took me from Mom and put me on the floor. After all that warm hugging, the floor felt cold.

I looked up at Dad, then towards Mom wondering what was happening. Since I'm still learning my own doggy language, I had no idea what people's babbling meant. My future Mom and Dad were saying something – although at times they looked down they mostly ignored me.

While the rest of my pack remained in our warm whelping kennel, I did not enjoy being all alone on that cold floor.

Looking up towards those giants standing next to me gave me an urge to escape. I needed some place that offered protection, and I moved quickly to scurry beneath a large couch. Now all I could see were Mom and Dad's feet. That was okay and offered some comfort.

It was a sad moment seeing their feet moving and finally walking away.

I didn't know something great had happened. While I was hiding, I guess my Mom and Dad said they loved me. They wanted me. There was no way, at that time, for me to know what Mom and Dad were saying, but that was the exact moment I was adopted.

For another week I remained with my siblings learning important doggy etiquette from my mother, Dory.

I played with my litter family until we were all dead-tired. Playing meant we nipped and yipped and did all sorts of puppy things. While we jumped and climbed over one another, we discovered the rules of safety. Feeling the pinch of a hard bite stopped all fun. None of us liked it. It didn't take very long before we all got the message it's acceptable to play hard – but play without hurting.

As for going, you know what I mean: peeing and pooping. At first, not knowing any better we wet and dirtied whenever and wherever the impulse hit. Sleeping near that smelly mess made all of us, especially me, very uncomfortable.

Of course we kept hearing the message to do our business, outside – in our yard. The backyard is just beyond the slider door. Although we kind of got the essence of that rule, and believe me, we tried to comply, but many times we would play and then waited just a bit too long – and, yep you guessed it, we didn't make it.

As I said earlier, my birth mother is named Dory. You may laugh and make fun of me, but I think she loved me the best. As an example, when I tried to feed she didn't kick me away like she did to my brothers and sisters. They were bigger, and much stronger than me. They would push and shove to feed first. Dory knew what they were doing. She made sure I got my share of her milk. I still dream of those days nestling up to Dory, feeling her warmth and sucking in the most luscious food in the world. While Dory mothered and nurtured her litter, Casper, my birth-father romped around the house and yard. He made a big effort to ignore us.

The day my Mom and Dad came to get me was both exciting and at the same time very frightening. I ran and peed with the excitement of seeing them again. Then we did the same ritual as last time: being hugged by Mom and Dad.

I realized something special was happening when Mom removed my collar. Oh that felt good getting rid of that ring from around my neck. It always bothered me and scratching would not relieve the itch. Now, Mom dressed me in a new pink and black halter. As I said I never liked that collar – this new halter gave me a cuddly feeling of security. After dressing, my Dad and Mom held me and asked for a first family photo.

Mitzi rolling in laughter

First family picture - 9 weeks

From my perspective, this was way too much activity. Compared to the usual visits, after a few minutes of grabbing and pawing us, people would leave.

At nine weeks old, I am the last of my litter to say goodbye to my birthing home.

I've been in a car before so this wasn't a new experience. In the past, I was always in a box with my brothers and sisters. This time Mom was holding me as Dad drove us away. This was way different. My heart pounded. I squirmed trying to look back to where I don't know, but my place of comfort was somewhere back there. Mom cooed and talked to me in a soothing voice. Her cuddling made me settle-in and nest in her arms. I could hear the steady beat of her heart. It calmed my high sense of panic down to a mere deep anxiety. The hum of the car rolling along offered me a little soothing gentle rocking, and at the same time kept me aware that I'm in for a big surprise.

Our car stopped next to a huge building; a large door in the wall moved up allowing Dad an opening to drive into what would become my new home. Mom still held me while Dad exited the car. He came around to Mom's door and lifted me from the comfort of her arms.

A new long leash attached to my halter gave me some freedom. I walked like a big girl from the parked car, out of the garage into an open area of pavement and grass. A scent hit me. I had to relieve my system and released a stream of urine. Hearing Mom and Dad saying I was a good-girl sounded great, but I didn't know what for.

After reentering the building we stepped into and out of an elevator. I now know what an elevator is, but, back then it was like going into a closet, and a minute later walking out again. Exiting on the fifth floor and a short distance away was the doorway to my new home.

The scents and odors within Condo 503 hit my sensitive nose. I twitched and sniffed in an attempt to recognize something, anything – to no avail.

Even at my young age of nine weeks, I understood a basic goal. This place, if it is my new home needed some marking. I took care of that almost immediately. Once I had the freedom to run, I returned to the entranceway and tried hard to pee making a tiny puddle just inside the doorway. Then I ran to the far end of the condo. I was squeezing as hard as I could and successfully wet again creating another very tiny slick of moisture – just inside the slider in the living room.

Mom and Dad were lucky they didn't give me access to the master bedroom, or the guest bedroom, or I would have enjoyed adding my scent to those as well – that is if I could have forced out another drop or two.

Seeing my new parents scurrying with paper towels was a real hoot. They could wipe away the dampness, but my marks are there forever.

As to pooping, when the urge came a few hours later, as a matter of consistency, I made certain to hit the same spots I used earlier.

Mom and Dad made a fuss, but a little encouragement was all that was necessary for me to understand I had my own personal sanitary disposal area.

People may call them training pads. I call it my en-suite facility. The fun part is the ado Mom and Dad make when they change the pad. They call me good-girl and offer me a special yummy treat. Dad will gather the soiled pad and I'll sit and wait, very patiently near the kitchen trashcan. Once that lid is closed my treat is moments away – yummy.

The pad is always there, and I use it on occasion. My three-times-a-day walks just about take care of any need to eliminate. I guess using a pad is part of growing up.

Getting back to my first day in my new home – it was terrible. All my life, for all nine weeks, I had company with my littermates, or with Dory. We shared our warmth and slept without fear. Now I have my own crate, and it is a nice crate with a terrific bed all soft and sweet smelling. On that first night, with all the lights out and all alone in a crate, within a small walled-in kennel, gave me the shivers. I cried and cried until Dad came, picked me up and hugged me. I felt a little better. I stopped whimpering. After a few minutes of cuddling, he again left me alone. I did not like that.

Mini-kennel with crate

It felt the same as when my littermates started to leave. Their warmth left me. Having Dory to lean against gave some satisfaction, but she did not want me to suckle, and she would jump out of the kennel. Back then I was never ever really alone. Casper and Dory were always just beyond the whelping kennel.

Mom and Dad kept coming back to comfort me during that ugly first night in my new home. I know none of us got any sleep.

During the next few nights, they tried a lot of different ways to make me feel at home. Eventually, Dad removed the fence that made a wall for the kennel. Bye-bye kennel. Then they moved my bed, which was in the crate, and placed it next to the doorway of Mom and Dad's bedroom. Mom covered my own personal little den with a big towel.

Now I loved it. It was a wonderful snug place all of my own. My bed, with pillow edges all around filled the bottom of the crate. I had a nice comfy soft edge to either nestle against or rest my head on top.

Mitzi at home in her den (crate)

Although Mom and Dad closed their bedroom during the nighttime, I could hear and smell them. I love them, and I felt safe and happy.

With the kennel enclosure gone it gave me the freedom to roam the living room, dining room, kitchen and den. My folks did something I really appreciate: they installed the pee pad near the hall doorway of the den. And a light next to the pad is always on. As I said before I learned really fast they were very pleased and rewarded me with a treat every time I used the pad. It didn't matter whether I wet or dirtied I got those delicious treats. Sometimes when I yearned for a munchie I tried to squeeze out a little wet – it worked most of the time. They would laugh at my attempt and seemed to enjoy my game for getting a goody.

I love being part of everything and the easiest way to capture Mom and Dad's attention is to wait until they're eating and beg for food. Sneaking up and nestling into their lap works wonders, especially when I keep my eyes open wide and allow my tongue to show a tiny bit. It always gets to them. At first, they would pet me and break off a smidge of their meal. Taking it very gently then retreating is good for a couple of rounds, from each, then hearing a gruff reprimand tells me that's it and to rest under the table. Of course, I would try again. It works about half of the time. Don't get me wrong. My people feed me the best, and I love the kibble they buy. It's just fun to beg and stir up the folks. Hey, they have to know I'm around.

But I'm getting ahead of my story. The first few weeks were difficult for me, for Mom and for Dad. They tried to satisfy my needs – and they did, for the most part. At my age of ten weeks, I was still a baby. I had a lot to learn. I was growing. My coat was getting longer, and growing and growing. Getting brushed and combed seemed to me an unnecessary trauma. My hair tangled and when they pulled the comb through it hurt. Seeing the comb and brush was a signal to me, to run, and hide.

Now keeping my coat clean meant, at times, some extra wiping of my rear end – after we came back from our walk. Oh, I meant to tell you I learned very quickly that our three times a day walk had a serious purpose. They gave me a treat when I wet or dirtied outside. I heard many words of praise from both Mom and Dad. They truly were happy when I did my duty while outside. They were pleased, and I got a reward.

Even though I know when it is time, Dad always asked if I want to go out. Sure I want to go out, but I hold back a little waiting for a goody. He puts his hand down, and I trot over take a tasty morsel from him. A moment later, I get hoisted up onto the dressing table. Oh yes, I have a dressing table. All of my halters, collars, leashes, supplies for grooming are on a table in the center of the den. Yeah, the combs and brushes are there too, and I always get a hair-do before they slip on a halter.

I like the halters better than the collars. I can tug and pull without feeling any pressure on my throat. Most of the time, I wear halters. However, I know when I get too rambunctious the Martingale collar will be used the next time out. That Martingale collar fits perfectly and has a release that allows it to open up. It offers no pressure unless the leash is pulled taunt. At least, it is not a choker collar that I see on some other dogs during our walks.

I love our walks, and I keep meeting new friends. One of my first and best friends is Mazy. She is a big Golden Retriever. When we get together we play really hard. As I said she's big, and at times she gets a little too rough. Mazy is a great role model for me. When we first met, I knew I wanted to be just like her. She can run free do her duty and romp around. Mazy even carries her own leash while walking. I love Mazy.

Mitzi at 3 months

Before I came to my new home I joined my siblings for a visit to the vet. I did not enjoy that. None of us did. We yipped and complained with the needle sticks and hoped that would never again happen. Ha, was I mistaken.

One of the first car rides I had, other than when I first came home was another appointment to the vet. This time he sat on the floor and encouraged me to join him. It was like playtime. He wasn't a threat and handled me gently.

I wasn't too pleased with his assistant when she took me in the back room and clipped my nails. That I didn't like then, and I don't like it now. And I don't want to talk about my spaying experience, period. Forget I mentioned the subject.

Talk about fun. I love to chew. When I first came home I wanted to chew on most things. Table legs were a real favorite until Mom told me that furniture-chewing was a big NO-NO. I don't do that anymore. Now I have a nice collection of chewable toys that my folks bought for me.

Some toys are very hard. Some are super soft but kind of strong. There is one that looks like a squirrel. Soon as I saw it I knew it was a dummy. They even sewed in squeakers that make a noise when I bite or stomp on it. I hate those squeakers and work hard to rip the toy open and get rid of those plastic noise makers.

Mom grumbles when she finds bits of the squeakers on the floor.

Mitzi loves to chew her toys

The best part in using some of my toys is playing tug with Dad. Oh does he hang on – and pulls – and then spins me around. It's when I win, or maybe when Dad thinks he lets me win, gives me a good feeling.

Dragging a toy around is no fun. So I flip it into the air and let it bounce, sometimes it lands on me – and then I grab it again. Sometime this teases Dad and he reaches for it. Dancing back and forth with any toy in my mouth, while in front of Mom and Dad, seems to make them happy. Anyhow, I think it makes them happy and that makes me happy.

I have other toys. They are stored in my own private toy box. It usually stays in its place, in the dining room, right next to the bookcase. Everything in this box is mine. Any time I want I can dig through and find what looks like a special.

Right now I have four different sized balls. Each is a special toy. The bright yellow tennis ball, with its hairy cover, is easy to pick up and carry. I just have to get a pinch of that cover and lug the ball where ever I want. The other balls are much smaller with shiny covers. They can be nosed to push or mouthed to carry. I get extra fun from these by rolling them under the couch and barking. Mom and Dad yell and storm at the noise I'm making then they realize I lost something, and they try to retrieve it.

It takes a little effort to train your parents – even if I have to say it myself, I'm pretty good at it.

I have a huge soccer ball and a bright red beach ball. Both of those are impossible to carry. But they are great fun to nose around the house.

I know they enjoy it and every once in the while I have to play with my folks. They always respond to an invitation to play toss-the-ball. They're good at it and can heave the smaller ball over my head and all the way down the hallway. I'll yip and chase after it. Running back with ball in my mouth, and flying past the waiting hands of Dad or Mom is fun. Hearing them encouraging me to come back to them is a real laugher. Eventually

I'll give in, come close allowing Dad an opportunity to grab the ball. For the few moments I have it, I can slobber it with the moisture in my mouth then get Dad's hands slick before letting the ball go. Now that is a blast. One thing I can't understand is why they dry the ball with a tissue before tossing it again down the hall.

Did I tell you about the treat toy? It is a small black circle of rubber made to look like a car tire. Just like a regular tire it is hollow in the center, and that's where Mom stuffs goodies. This is a unique deal that I receive only when they are going out – out without me. They know I hate to hear the word STAY. So I guess they feel guilty about leaving me all alone to protect our home and offer this gem of a stuffed toy.

I never know what's in the tire. When they roll it towards me, I get a whiff of an idea.

Working on breaking the stuffing free gives me a continuing tease of smell and taste. No big bites but a lot of tidbits. After the last gulp is safely in my belly, then the condo is mine to enjoy.

Being all alone is okay. It is an opportunity to explore, especially if they forget to close the bedroom doors. An open bedroom door usually means an open bathroom door, which means a chance to search through all the dirty laundry.

Socks are my main target. I can grab one of those and chew until the entire thing is in my mouth – and get it all sopping wet. Playing with one sock is never enough and I know if I find one, there are more to be had.

And as all smart dogs know, we have to hide our newly found possessions. Although I've tried, Mom always traces my path and finds my treasures.

Mitzi at one year

So that's me, Mitzi. I have a lot more to tell like the time I went to school. Yep, I'm an educated pup. It was a lot of fun going to classes. I was just about six months old when I started a course. Attending the lessons didn't train me but taught my Dad how to work with me. They called it Obedience Training. I call it snack time.

For eight weeks, we joined a group of seven other dogs in these fun sessions. It was a great time. The instructor told all the owners to reward their pet anytime we did sometime right. I don't know why they didn't give Dad something when he did all the work. The teacher made the rules. I enjoyed the lessons and tried to mimic the teacher's dog. That way I made sure I received the yummy.

For our final exam, I could sit, go down, and walk next to Dad. Our trainer said I was extremely smart – and I graduated.

We didn't always go to the school to learn something new. Dad and Mom worked with me teaching different tricks. I'm not talking about playtime. Playing together is always fun but that doesn't mean I'd get a treat. I have to do something extraordinary before getting a reward.

**Mitzi working with the
hurdles and hoop**

This time they wanted me to leap over
hurdles. Dad made a set of hurdles out of plastic

pipe. They also wanted me to jump through a hoop. Mom said it was a kid-sized hula-hoop. Okay, I thought, let's do it. This is not a big deal. I can jump and do what I need to do to get to where I want to go.

So when we started I decided to do silly things like instead of jumping I'd dance around the hurdles. Watching their reaction was a real laugher. Seeing Dad's hand going into the treat bag brought a big smile to my face. Yes, I can smile if you would only notice. Well, that hand in the bag tempted me. I looked up in anticipation, but he didn't offer any. So I did a small jump, not over it, but closer to the hurdle. Again, I looked up to see their reaction. Mom offered a half of a dog-biscuit. These are the real tiny size. And at the same time she sang some words praising my attempt. Hmm, I got a half a treat for a near miss. What would happen if I actually jumped over the hurdle?

Mom is very consistent and always insists that I sit before beginning any trick or whatever. She may want that, but it is far more fun for me that when she says to sit, I drop into a down position – with my back legs sticking straight out. My belly is on the floor. My chin is on the floor. Mom keeps repeating sit, sit, and I merely look up at her and smile. There I go again – smiling. You have to remember if I did everything correct right away, the game, or lesson would end quickly. I need and want their attention, and I get it by my delaying tactics.

I know eventually I have to sit to satisfy Mom's need to teach me the new trick. So I sat and I jumped over the hurdle, and they shouted praise and cheered my performance. And as I thought, I received a full-sized tasty biscuit. A couple of chomps broke it into swallowing bits, and I'm ready for another command.

They encouraged me to jump over one hurdle then two hurdles in a row. Satisfied that I had those tricks mastered Dad brought out a hoop showing it to me like I never saw a hoop before. I sniffed it to show some interest. Then apparently doubting my ability or desire to go through the hoop Mom had it touching the floor. I could walk through it. Knowing that wouldn't earn a reward, without any prompting I jumped right through the middle. I guessed right and received another treat. Now we're both happy.

I don't understand humans. They get all excited thinking I'm learning something different. Most of the time I know how, I just don't know when they want me to do these things.

Since we're talking about tricks, Terry, one of Mom & Dad's daughters, showed me how to run around a table when she pointed the route. That stunt was a little unusual, and she had to lead the way. Once I got it, I realized that go-around is one of my favorite commands. The problem with this routine, I have to run and work too hard for a tiny tasty morsel. No, I am not spoiled. I can have an opinion can't I?

y home is perfect. I just wish I could always sleep in my own bed, in my own crate, and where it is most of the time.

During the hurricane Matthew, Mom and Dad took me, crate, bed and all to Jean and John's house. Jean is another daughter of Mom and Dad. As you can see I have a big and beautiful adopted family. And part of Jean's family is three grown-up dachshunds. To be fair this was their home, we were guests, but those pups sure made me uncomfortable.

The moment I entered their home, they, with Louie leading the pack, chased me right into the big swimming pool. I didn't even know what a pool was until I tried running into it, and suddenly I was airborne and landed in deep water.

No one ever taught me how to swim, and this instant plunge made me dig down deep into my survival instincts. I paddled with my four legs going like thunder towards Jean. She had jumped into the pool, shoes and all then reached out to me scooping me up into her arms. I was soaking wet and a little cold.

It felt good getting a brisk rubdown as Mom tried to dry my coat with a big fluffy towel.

Now those three dachshunds knew what they did, and they enjoyed teasing me. Lucy and Maxine were kind of social but Louie was alpha-dog all the way. This was his turf, and he made certain I understood. I had to hide or stay with Mom and Dad during the storm.

As for this hurricane, it made a lot of noise – just not enough to keep me awake all night. I curled up in my own wonderful cozy crate and two days later we returned home.

I don't like hurricanes, and I've lived through two of them. After Matthew, we had to escape from hurricane Irma. This time Mom and Dad left me with a nice bunch of women, and I stayed at a Dog Motel. It was okay. I had my own living area with one of my beds plopped in the corner. The only problem, this storm hit hard and the entire kennel lost all power. We stayed in the dark all night. The women remained with us, and it was sort of party time with a lot of huddle and cuddle.

I'll say it again, I don't like hurricanes; and I hate going to the kennel.

I Stayed at another kennel while Mom and Dad took a little cruise. This new place was sleek and modern with a great open area for dogs my size. We could run and play and do our business while one attendant always watched making certain the bullies didn't get a chance to push us around.

I have to admit being away gives me a chance to meet new people and be with dogs my size.

We live in a condo right on the beach. I've been on the beach and walked on hot and dusty sand as well as cold and wet sand.

Waves coming in are a challenge for me, and I don't like getting wet. I usually can hear the waves before I'm in trouble. Of course, there is a law that says I, and my kind, are not allowed on the beach, at any time. The dog catcher patrols and at times nabs some of my friends. Their owners have to pay a lot of money when they are caught.

They can keep the beach. I'd rather walk on the nice sidewalk. I should say I rather walk on the sidewalk when it is early morning or at nighttime – just before it gets dark. It is very comfortable, especially when the wind blows. And believe me the wind is very interesting as it comes in off or going towards the ocean. I love to point my nose into the breeze and catch all the smells. Ah – that is pure joy.

Another delight of mine is riding in the car – most of the time. Mom holds me on her lap, and I can see out the front window or if something is of interest watch it go by using the side windows.

I said most of the time because I don't like going to the groomer, and I don't like going to the kennel, and I don't like going to the vet, and I don't – I guess you get the idea that there are places that I just don't care for. So when we get into the car, I never know if it's for a nice ride or ta-da here we go again.

Riding for a long time can get boring, and when that happens, I try to slip off Mom's lap and get down to the floor. That space is nice and dark, and I can curl up and get in between Mom's feet.

Scratching around trying to see what's beneath the rug is tempting. It is also a big No-No. Still at times I have to yield to my urges. Both Mom and Dad always chide my attempts to explore and seek out the mysteries under the rug.

I get a kick out of hearing their voices knowing they care about me.

If you think I'm rambling and switching thoughts, you're right. Just remember I'm two years old. My mind is always going at full speed. So bear with me as I continue to relate who I am and what I like.

There are three likes that are my favorites: I like to eat. I like to play, and I like to sleep; and pretty much in that order. Of course, there are other elements of my life that are important. I still like to eat, play, and sleep the best.

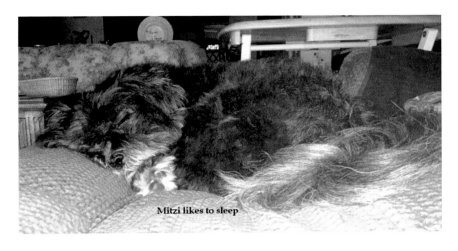

Mitzi likes to sleep

As for eating I get the finest. Mom buys Purina Beyond for Small Dogs. They call it kibble; I call it delicious and fun.

At times, Mom and Dad feed the kibble one piece at a time in a game of toss and catch. They toss it into the air, and if they do it right I catch it before it hits the ground. Sometimes the toss is beyond my ability to reach then I have to scurry to find it. This is a great game, and I never tire playing.

I always eat first. Then Mom and Dad try to have their meal sitting at the dining room table. While they're eating I usually take my place just under Mom's feet. When I think the timing is right I'll sneak a nose under the tablecloth and rest it on Mom's lap. Sometimes it works and sometimes it doesn't. They tell me their food isn't always good for me. It has to do with my belly's reaction to things like onions and garlic and avocados. There's a hold bunch of items that I should not eat. So they eat and I wonder what it is that they have, and I can't.

Mom and Dad can control what I eat at home. However, when we go out for a walk, I can spy a morsel on the ground and scoop it up before anyone can stop me. If I like the taste it's mine and I'll chomp and chew until I'm ready to swallow. Mom and Dad may try to take it from me but no way will I give it up. I hear them say it is dirty; I hear them say it could be something bad; I can hear them and I just continue chewing. If they make an attempt to open my mouth I just swallow and smile. Ha-Ha all gone.

My water bowl is washed and filled every morning – immediately after our walk. Walking for an hour makes me thirsty. I know the routine. We enter the condo, and I wait for that cool water from the refrigerator. I watch as my water bowl is filled and then lowered towards me. I start slurping before the bowl reaches the floor.

During my walks I meet a lot of human and dog friends. On occasion, I see a cat. Brother dogs and sister dogs I love – cats are too aloof for me.

I like to sniff and explore as I stroll. Too many times people get in my way and they want to touch me. Naturally I back away for self-protection; and sometimes I let out a low growl of warning. Dad doesn't like me growling so I try to keep my sentiments to myself and move away.

Don't misunderstand me; I connect with a lot of different folks. There are many people I love.

Take a guy named Turtle. He lives in his '86 Volkswagen camper and goes wherever life leads him. When he drives-by he toots his horn and I woof back.

Mom and Dad know many of the people we meet on our walks – and most of them have a dog on a lead. Here are the names of some of my friends; Kenneth, Mazy, Katie, Charlie, Harry, Talley, Pippy, Sadie, Socks, Cookie and Maverick. Cookie and Maverick live in our building and I see them very often. Maverick loves to run and we get along great.

Although we live in Florida, on occasion we have very cold weather – and rainy days. I love the cold days. I get to wear my beautiful sweater. Pulling it on over my head is no fun because I hate having my eyes covered with anything. Once it is on, it cuddles my back and belly; I feel warm; I feel safe. Mom says the sweater is an argyle knit in pink and black – whatever that is.

If it rains, I get to wear my yellow slicker with an attached hood. I have to slip my head into the hood before the slicker covers my back.

Ready for the chilly days

When we walk, I continually try to shake the hood off; Dad keeps pushing it back. Walking in the rain is fun. My paws splash in all the puddles getting my belly very wet. As for my tail, it catches the rain as it falls, and sometimes it gets wet from the splashes I make with my feet.

By the time we get home I'm dripping wet with water– but most of my back is dry. I leave a trail of dripping moisture as we enter the building.

ready for the rainy days

A great towel rub is the best part of walking in the rain. It gets me dry and makes me very sleepy. By this time I am ready for nap.

Most people would say I live, with my family, in a condo on the beach. I look at it differently. The condo is my den, and I am alpha-dog with two humans. In my pack I assign the status and identify each by scent – in my dog's world, we don't have names.

Since people have a very limited ability to smell, and I can't describe the complexity of my Mom and Dad's scents I can only tell you how I relate to them. Keep in mind I'm telling Dad which type of symbol to use for each of them. Hopefully, it will give you some idea of how I think. My parents are ♥ and OXO. Can you guess* which one is Mom and which one is Dad – and why?

I left you some *clues** within my story.

Mitzi at two years

I hope you enjoyed my tale. And while you are pondering the how to find the solution to that little puzzle, just remember:

"My Name is Mitzi"

*Hint: *See* pages 7 & 8

Acknowledgement

Many thanks to our dear Mitzi for her love and patience. She came into our lives with all the excitement and enthusiasm only a baby puppy can exhibit. Mitzi adjusted well and is a daily reminder in all the joys a dog offers to their adopted family. Mitzi wants to be the alpha dog with us as members of her pack. That creates wonder after wonder how we humans and she as a canine learn to live together as a family. We love her dearly and she offers her own version of love every moment of every day.

As with all my writing I could not do any of it without the encouragement, editorial skills, and the perpetual support of my dear Marie. I never tire of the idea that my works are dedicated to my Marie.

About the Author

Frank J. Kopet, a retired Aerospace Corporation Division Manager, lives with his dear wife Marie, and their pup Mitzi, on the east coast of Florida.

Also by Frank J. Kopet

Justice Series
Grey Justice
A Touch of Love

Tomorrow Series
Wait 'Til Tomorrow
Wait 'Til Tomorrow II
Wait 'Til Tomorrow III
Sarah's Tomorrow

Website: www.frankjkopet.com

Email address: fjkopet@hotmail.com

I know I made some silly errors in
my book – like on pages 30 and 46.
You have to remember I'm a two
year old pup.
Love always – MITZI

Made in the USA
San Bernardino, CA
26 May 2018